Crafting Compelling Characters

Welcome to "Crafting Compelling Characters," a short creative writing course designed to help you develop rich and memorable characters for your stories. Whether you're an aspiring novelist, playwright, screenwriter, or just looking to improve your storytelling skills, this course will equip you with the tools and techniques to breathe life into your characters.

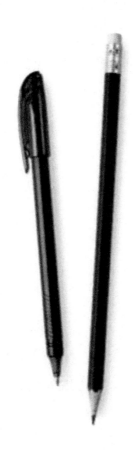

Course Objectives:

1. Understand the importance of well-developed characters in storytelling.
2. Explore various methods for creating multidimensional characters.
3. Learn how to build character backgrounds, motivations, and flaws.
4. Develop skills in writing authentic dialogue and character actions.
5. Gain insight into character arcs and growth throughout a story.

Session 1
Introduction to Character Development

Protagonists

❑ Protagonists are often the central characters of a story.

❑ They serve as the audience's entry point into the narrative, offering a perspective to relate to or root for.

❑ Protagonists typically undergo character development or transformation throughout the story, making their journey a source of emotional investment for the audience.

Antagonists

• Antagonists provide conflict and opposition to the protagonists.

• They challenge the protagonists' goals and beliefs, driving the plot's tension.

• Well-developed antagonists add depth to the story by offering alternative viewpoints or moral dilemmas.

Supporting Characters

- Supporting characters play various roles, from providing comic relief to offering guidance and wisdom.

- They contribute to the story's richness by adding diverse perspectives and interactions.

- Supporting characters can help reveal the protagonists' traits and motivations through their relationships.

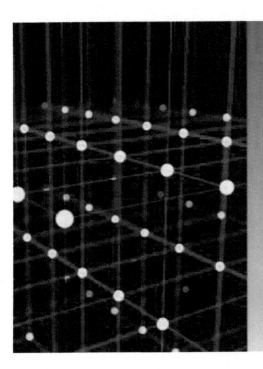

Catalysts

- Catalysts
- Catalysts initiate or accelerate the story's events.
- They introduce conflict or incite change, pushing the characters to take action.
- Catalysts are instrumental in propelling the plot forward and creating narrative momentum.

Setting as a Character

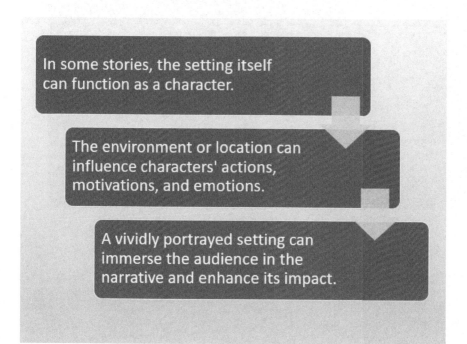

In some stories, the setting itself can function as a character.

The environment or location can influence characters' actions, motivations, and emotions.

A vividly portrayed setting can immerse the audience in the narrative and enhance its impact.

Exercise

Reflect on a character you are currently developing or an existing character from a favourite book or movie.

Jot down key details about their character, including their name, age, physical appearance, personality traits, backstory, and motivations.

Character's name

*

Character's age

*

Character's physical appearance

*

Character's personality traits.

*

Character's backstory.

*

Character's motivations.

How characters drive the plot and engage the reader

Well-crafted characters are the lifeblood of storytelling, and their presence can profoundly enhance the reader's experience in several ways: Emotional Connection: Readers form emotional bonds with characters who feel genuine, relatable, and multidimensional. When characters have distinct personalities, vulnerabilities, and emotions, readers can empathize with their struggles, joys, and challenges. This emotional connection makes readers care deeply about the characters' fates and the overall story.

Engagement

Characters are the driving force behind the plot. Well-developed characters make readers invested in the story's unfolding events because they want to see how these characters will navigate and grow through challenges. Readers become active participants in the narrative, eagerly turning pages to discover what happens next.

~*~

Complexity: Multi-layered characters add depth and complexity to the story. Just like real people, well-crafted characters have flaws, strengths, contradictions, and evolving beliefs. This complexity makes characters more interesting and relatable, as readers can see aspects of themselves or people they know in the characters' struggles and growth.

Themes and Messages

Characters can embody and explore thematic elements of a story. Through their actions, choices, and conflicts, characters can represent broader ideas, social issues, or moral dilemmas. This allows readers to engage with and reflect upon these themes through the lens of the characters' experiences.

Suspense and Tension: Characters with distinct personalities and motivations can create internal and external conflicts within the story. These conflicts drive the narrative forward, creating suspense and tension that captivate the reader's attention. Readers become invested in resolving these conflicts and discovering how characters will overcome obstacles.

Session 2
Building Character Foundations

Character Backstories and Motivations

Motivation: A character's history often serves as the primary source of motivation. Past events and experiences can drive characters to pursue specific goals or take particular actions. For example, a character who has lost a loved one to a tragic accident might be motivated by a desire for justice or revenge.

Trauma: Past traumas can have a profound impact on a character's behavior. Traumatic events can lead to psychological scars, resulting in behaviours such as avoidance, aggression, or anxiety. Characters may make choices to cope with or confront their past traumas, and these choices can become central to the story's plot.

Beliefs and Values: A character's upbringing and cultural background are part of their history and can shape their beliefs and values. These beliefs influence their ethical code and guide their decision-making. A character's moral compass, for instance, might lead them to take heroic or villainous actions depending on their upbringing and personal history.

Fear and Insecurity: Characters often carry unresolved fears and insecurities from their past. These emotional wounds can affect their choices and actions, leading them to avoid certain situations or pursue others. Overcoming these fears can be a central character arc in a story.

Motivation

A character's history often serves as the primary source of motivation. Past events and experiences can drive characters to pursue specific goals or take particular actions. For example, a character who has lost a loved one to a tragic accident might be motivated by a desire for justice or revenge.

Trauma

Past traumas can have a profound impact on a character's behaviour. Traumatic events can lead to psychological scars, resulting in behaviours such as avoidance, aggression, or anxiety. Characters may make choices to cope with or confront their past traumas, and these choices can become central to the story's plot.

Beliefs and Values

A character's upbringing and cultural background are part of their history and can shape their beliefs and values. These beliefs influence their ethical code and guide their decision-making. A character's moral compass, for instance, might lead them to take heroic or villainous actions depending on their upbringing and personal history.

Fear and Insecurity

Characters often carry unresolved fears and insecurities from their past. These emotional wounds can affect their choices and actions, leading them to avoid certain situations or pursue others. Overcoming these fears can be a central character arc in a story.

Relationships: The history of a character's relationships, whether familial, romantic, or platonic, can significantly impact their actions and choices. Past conflicts, betrayals, or deep connections can drive characters to make decisions that either nurture or challenge these relationships.

Change and Growth: A character's history can be the foundation for their growth and development throughout the narrative. As characters confront their past mistakes or embrace their past achievements, they can evolve and change over the course of the story.

Secrets and Revelations: Hidden or undisclosed aspects of a character's history can create suspense and tension in a story. When secrets from a character's past are revealed, it can lead to unexpected actions and choices as they grapple with the consequences of their history coming to light.

Interactions with Other Characters: Characters' histories often intersect and clash with those of other characters. These intersections can lead to conflicts, alliances, or unexpected alliances based on shared or opposing past experiences.

In summary, histories are instrumental in creating complex, multidimensional characters. Understanding a character's past provides insight into their motivations, fears, beliefs, and values, all of which drive their actions and choices throughout the story. By weaving histories into the narrative, storytellers can craft more authentic and relatable characters and engage readers in the character's journey of growth, change, and self-discovery.

Relationships

The history of a character's relationships, whether familial, romantic, or platonic, can significantly impact their actions and choices. Past conflicts, betrayals, or deep connections can drive characters to make decisions that either nurture or challenge these relationships.

Change and Growth

A character's history can be the foundation for their growth and development throughout the narrative. As characters confront their past mistakes or embrace their past achievements, they can evolve and change over the course of the story.

Secrets and Revelations

Hidden or undisclosed aspects of a character's history can create suspense and tension in a story. When secrets from a character's past are revealed, it can lead to unexpected actions and choices as they grapple with the consequences of their history coming to light.

Interactions with Other Characters

Characters' histories often intersect and clash with those of other characters. These intersections can lead to conflicts, alliances, or unexpected alliances based on shared or opposing past experiences.

In summary, histories are instrumental in creating complex, multidimensional characters. Understanding a character's past provides insights into their motivations, fears, beliefs, and values, all of which drive their actions and choices throughout the story. By weaving histories into the narrative, storytellers can craft more authentic and relatable characters and engage readers in the character's journey of growth, change, and self-discovery.

Identifying core motivations and goals for your characters

❑ **Survival:** The primal instinct to survive can be a powerful motivation. Characters driven by survival may take extreme actions protect themselves or their loved ones when faced with danger or adversity.

❑ **Love and Connection:** Many characters are motivated by love, whether it's for a romantic partner, family member, or friend. desire for connection and emotional bonds can lead characters to make sacrifices or take risks to maintain these relationships.

❑ **Justice and Redemption:** Characters motivated by a sense of justice seek to right wrongs and bring about fairness. They may a personal vendetta or a strong moral compass that compels them to fight for what they believe is right.

❑ **Ambition and Success:** Some characters are driven by ambition and the pursuit of success. Whether it's achieving a career go gaining power, or accumulating wealth, their motivation lies in personal achievement and recognition.

❑ **Revenge:** Characters motivated by revenge are often fueled by past wrongs or injustices. Their actions are guided by a desire settle scores and seek vengeance against those who have harmed them or their loved ones.

Identifying core motivations and goals for your characters

❑ **Survival:** The primal instinct to survive can be a powerful motivation. Characters driven by survival may take extreme actions to protect themselves or their loved ones when faced with danger or adversity.

❑ **Love and Connection:** Many characters are motivated by love, whether it's for a romantic partner, family member, or friend. The desire for connection and emotional bonds can lead characters to make sacrifices or take risks to maintain these relationships.

❑ **Justice and Redemption:** Characters motivated by a sense of justice seek to right wrongs and bring about fairness. They may have a personal vendetta or a strong moral compass that compels them to fight for what they believe is right.

❑ **Ambition and Success:** Some characters are driven by ambition and the pursuit of success. Whether it's achieving a career goal, gaining power, or accumulating wealth, their motivation lies in personal achievement and recognition.

❑ **Revenge**: Characters motivated by revenge are often fueled by past wrongs or injustices. Their actions are guided by a desire to settle scores and seek vengeance against those who have harmed them or their loved ones.

Exercise

Exercise Title: "Exploring Character Core Motivations"

Objective: This exercise is designed to help writers and storytellers delve deeper into their characters' motivations and understand how these motivations drive their actions and decisions.

Materials Needed:
Writing materials (notebook, computer, or preferred writing tools)

Instructions:

Select a Character: Choose a character from your current writing project or create a new character for this exercise.

Identify Core Motivations: Take a moment to consider what drives your character at their core. What are their deepest desires, fears, and values? These are the motivations that guide their actions throughout the story.

List Motivations: Create a list of the character's core motivations. These motivations can be positive (e.g., love, justice) or negative (e.g., revenge, fear), and they can be a combination of both. Try to identify at least three core motivations.

Prioritize Motivations: Rank the motivations in order of importance to your character. Which one is the most significant? Which ones are secondary or tertiary motivations? This ranking will help you understand which motivations are the driving force behind their actions.

Write a Journal Entry: Imagine that your character is writing a journal entry or a personal reflection. In this entry, have the character discuss their motivations. Ask questions such as:

- ❑ Why do these motivations matter so much to them?
- ❑ How have these motivations evolved or changed over time?
- ❑ Have they made sacrifices or difficult choices because of these motivations?
- ❑ What would they be willing to do to achieve their most important motivation?

Write a Scene: Create a scene that showcases your character's core motivations in action. Place them in a situation where they must make a decision or take action based on one of their motivations. This scene should highlight the emotional and internal conflicts they may face.

Reflect and Analyze

After completing the scene, take a step back and analyze the character's actions and decisions. How did their motivations influence their choices? Did they stay true to their core motivations, or did they face internal conflicts? What consequences or conflicts arose as a result of their actions?

Repeat for Other Motivations

If you have identified multiple core motivations, repeat the exercise by creating additional scenes that explore how each motivation influences the character's choices.

Summarize Insights

In your writing journal or document, summarize the insights you gained about your character's core motivations and how they impact the story. Consider how these motivations will shape the character's arc and relationships with other characters.

This exercise allows writers to dig deep into their characters' motivations and gain a better understanding of what drives them. It can lead to more authentic character development and help writers create compelling and multidimensional characters in their stories.

❏ **Select a Character:** Choose a character from your current writing project or create a new character for this exercise.

❏ **Identify Core Motivations:** Take a moment to consider what drives your character at their core. What are their deepest desires, fears, and values? These are the motivations that guide their actions throughout the story.

❏ **List Motivations:** Create a list of the character's core motivations. These motivations can be positive (e.g., love, justice) or negative (e.g., revenge, fear), and they can be a combination of both. Try to identify at least three core motivations.

❏ **Prioritize Motivations:** Rank the motivations in order of importance to your character. Which one is the most significant? Which ones are secondary or tertiary motivations? This ranking will help you understand which motivations are the driving force behind their actions.

Session 3
Creating Complex Characters

❑ **Select a Character:** Choose a character from your current writing project or create a new character for this exercise.

~*~

❑ **Identify Core Motivations:** Take a moment to consider what drives your character at their core. What are their deepest desires, fears, and values? These are the motivations that guide their actions throughout the story.

~*~

❑ **List Motivations:** Create a list of the character's core motivations. These motivations can be positive (e.g., love, justice) or negative (e.g., revenge, fear), and they can be a combination of both. Try to identify at least three core motivations.

~*~

❑ **Prioritize Motivations:** Rank the motivations in order of importance to your character. Which one is the most significant? Which ones are secondary or tertiary motivations? This ranking will help you understand which motivations are the driving force behind their actions.

Flaws and Imperfections

- How character flaws add depth and relatability.
- Balancing strengths and weaknesses in your characters.

How character flaws add depth and relatability.

Character flaws are essential elements of storytelling that add depth and relatability to characters. They serve to humanize characters, making them more believable and engaging to readers or viewers. Here's why character flaws are so important in character development.

Realism: In real life, nobody is perfect. Everyone has their quirks, weaknesses, and imperfections. When characters exhibit flaws, it mirrors the complexities of human nature. Readers can relate to characters who are flawed because they see a reflection of themselves or people they know.

Conflict and Tension: Flaws often drive conflicts in a story. Whether it's a character's stubbornness, impulsiveness, or arrogance, these flaws can lead to misunderstandings, disagreements, and obstacles that create tension and drama. This conflict is a crucial ingredient for a compelling narrative.

Character Growth: Character flaws provide a platform for character growth and development. As characters grapple with their weaknesses, they have the potential to evolve and change over the course of the story. This transformation can be a powerful and satisfying arc for readers, as they witness the character's journey towards self-improvement.

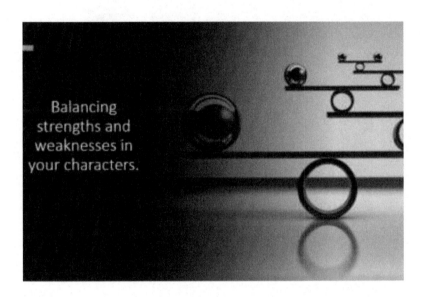

Balancing
strengths and
weaknesses in
your characters.

Balancing strengths and weaknesses in your characters is crucial for creating well-rounded, relatable, and interesting individuals in your stories. Here are some tips on how to achieve that balance:

Start with a Character Profile

Before you begin writing, create a detailed character profile. This should include not only their strengths and weaknesses but also their background, motivations, fears, desires, and personality traits. Having a comprehensive understanding of your character will help you identify the right balance.

Consider the Story's Needs

Think about the role your character plays in the story. What functions do they serve? How do their strengths and weaknesses impact the plot? Ensure that their attributes align with the narrative and contribute to its development.

Avoid Clichés

Steer clear of overused character stereotypes. Instead of giving your detective character the stereotypical "flaw" of being a loner or having a substance abuse problem, consider more unique and character-specific weaknesses that fit the context of your story.

Make Weaknesses Consequential

Ensure that your character's weaknesses have consequences. These consequences can drive the plot forward, create conflict, and offer opportunities for character growth. If a character's flaws don't impact the story in meaningful ways, they may feel superficial.

Show Growth and Change

Allow your characters to evolve over the course of the story. As they confront their weaknesses and learn from their experiences, they should grow and change. This character development is a powerful way to engage readers.

Balance Strengths with Vulnerabilities

Even when characters possess strengths, they should have vulnerabilities that can be exploited. This vulnerability could be emotional, psychological, or related to their values. It makes the character more relatable and adds tension to the story.

Create Internal Conflict

The best characters often grapple with internal conflicts stemming from their strengths and weaknesses. For example, a highly intelligent character might struggle with social relationships because they find it hard to relate to others. This internal conflict adds depth.

Use Foils

Introduce other characters who complement or contrast with your main character's strengths and weaknesses. This can create interesting dynamics and highlight aspects of your character's personality that may not otherwise be apparent.

Get Feedback

Share your character profiles and early drafts with beta readers or writing groups. They can provide valuable insights into whether your character's strengths and weaknesses feel balanced and authentic.

Consider the Character's Arc

Think about where you want your character to start and where you want them to end up. How will their strengths and weaknesses play a role in this character arc? Ensuring alignment between their development and their attributes is key to balance.

Avoid Perfection

Characters who are too flawless can be uninteresting and unrealistic. Likewise, characters who are nothing but weaknesses may frustrate readers. Seek a middle ground that reflects the complexities of human nature.

Remember that balance doesn't mean equality. Your character's strengths and weaknesses don't have to be perfectly matched. In fact, some imbalance can create intrigue and tension. Ultimately, the goal is to create characters who feel authentic, dynamic, and relatable to your readers.

Session 4
Breathing Life into Characters

Dialogue
and
Actions

Writing authentic dialogue
that reveals character
traits.

Showcasing characters
through their actions and
decisions.

Dialogue and Actions

❑   Writing authentic dialogue that reveals character traits.

❑   Showcasing characters through their actions and decisions.

Writing authentic dialogue that reveals character traits.

Writing authentic dialogue that reveals character traits is a crucial skill for bringing your characters to life in your stories. Here are some tips on how to do it effectively:

Know Your Characters Well

Before writing dialogue, have a deep understanding of your characters. Know their backgrounds, motivations, fears, desires, values, and flaws. The more you know about them, the easier it is to make their dialogue authentic and revealing of their unique traits.

Voice and Diction

Each character should have their own distinct voice and style of speaking. Consider factors like their education, upbringing, regional dialect, and social background. Use appropriate vocabulary and sentence structures that reflect these aspects of their identity.

Show, Don't Tell

Instead of directly telling the reader what a character is like, show it through their words and actions. For example, if a character is arrogant, have them speak in a condescending tone or use words that demonstrate their superiority.

Use Subtext

People often don't say exactly what they mean. Use subtext to add depth to your dialogue. Characters might have hidden agendas, concealed emotions, or unspoken tensions that can be revealed through what they don't say or through subtle hints.

Conflict and Tension

Dialogue is a great tool for showcasing conflicts and tensions between characters. These conflicts can arise from differences in values, goals, or personalities. Use dialogue to let these tensions surface naturally.

Reactions and Responses

Pay attention to how characters react to each other's dialogue. This can reveal a lot about their relationships and individual traits. For instance, a character who always responds aggressively to criticism may have an insecurity issue.

Consistency

Ensure that your characters' dialogue remains consistent with their established traits throughout the story. Sudden changes in speech patterns or behaviours can confuse readers and make characters seem inconsistent.

Use Dialogue Tags Sparingly

While dialogue tags (e.g., "he said," "she exclaimed") are necessary to indicate who is speaking, use them sparingly. Well-written dialogue should convey the tone and emotion of a conversation without relying heavily on tags.

Eavesdrop and Observe

Listen to real conversations and observe how people interact. Pay attention to the nuances of speech, body language, and the unspoken communication between individuals. This can provide valuable insights into crafting authentic dialogue.

Read Aloud

After writing dialogue, read it aloud to yourself. Does it sound natural? Does it fit the character's personality? Reading aloud can help you identify awkward or forced dialogue.

Edit and Revise

Dialogue often benefits from multiple rounds of editing. During revisions, focus on refining the dialogue to make it more authentic and character-revealing.

Beta Readers and Feedback

Share your work with beta readers or writing groups and ask for feedback specifically on the authenticity of your characters' dialogue. Fresh perspectives can help you identify areas for improvement.

Avoid Info Dumps

While dialogue can reveal character traits, avoid using it solely as a vehicle for conveying information or backstory. Make sure that character traits revealed through dialogue serve the broader narrative.

Writing authentic dialogue that reveals character traits takes practice, but it's a skill that can greatly enhance your storytelling. By immersing yourself in your characters' personalities and staying attuned to the subtleties of human communication, you can create dialogue that feels genuine and engaging to your readers.

Showcasing characters through their actions and decisions.

Showcasing characters through their actions and decisions is a powerful way to reveal their personalities, motivations, and growth throughout your story. Here are some tips on how to effectively achieve this:

Establish Clear Character Traits

Before you start writing, have a clear understanding of each character's unique traits, values, strengths, and weaknesses. Consider how these traits influence their actions and decisions.

Align Actions with Traits

Ensure that characters' actions are consistent with their established traits. For example, if you've established a character as compassionate, show them helping others or displaying empathy in various situations.

Motivation and Goals

Characters' actions should be driven by their motivations and goals. Understand what each character wants and what they are willing to do to achieve those goals. This will inform their decisions and actions.

Conflict and Obstacles

Introduce conflicts and obstacles that force characters to make decisions. These challenges can reveal their problem-solving skills, priorities, and values. Consider how characters react under pressure.

Consequences

Actions have consequences. Show how characters deal with the repercussions of their choices. This can highlight their resilience, adaptability, and ability to learn from their mistakes.

Internal Struggles

Characters may have internal conflicts that influence their actions and decisions. This could include moral dilemmas, doubts, or conflicting desires. Explore how these internal struggles impact their choices.

Dialogue and Inner Thoughts

Use dialogue and inner monologues to provide insight into characters' thoughts and motivations. Readers can gain a deeper understanding of why characters make certain decisions.

Symbolic Actions

Consider using symbolic actions to convey deeper meaning or foreshadow events. For example, a character who plants a garden might symbolize their desire for growth and renewal.

Character Arcs

Plan how characters will evolve over the course of the story. Show their growth by having their actions and decisions change as they learn and develop. This transformation should align with the character arc you've designed.

Contrast and Foil

Compare and contrast characters by placing them in similar situations. This can highlight their differences in values, priorities, and approaches to problem-solving.

Surprise Readers

Occasionally, have characters make unexpected decisions or take actions that challenge their established traits. This can create intrigue and keep readers engaged.

Balance Consistency with Change

While consistency is important, characters should also evolve and adapt as the story progresses. Balance their core traits with the need for growth and development.

Beta Readers and Feedback

Share your work with beta readers or writing groups and ask for feedback on whether the characters' actions and decisions feel authentic and consistent with their personalities.

Revisions

During the editing process, revisit your characters' actions and decisions to ensure they serve the story's purpose and contribute to character development.

By focusing on how characters' actions and decisions reflect their personalities, goals, and values, you can create well-rounded and dynamic characters that resonate with your readers. These choices not only advance the plot but also provide valuable insights into the human elements of your story.

Session 5
Character Arcs and Growth

Character Development Over the Course of a Story

- Exploring the concept of character arcs.
- How characters change and evolve throughout the narrative.

Exploring the concept of character arcs. Exploring the concept of character arcs is a fundamental aspect of storytelling. A character arc is the journey and transformation a character undergoes throughout a story. Here's how to effectively explore and incorporate character arcs into your writing:

Understand the Basics of Character Arcs

Start by familiarizing yourself with the three main types of character arcs: positive change, negative change, and flat arcs.

Positive change arcs involve characters who evolve and grow, overcoming flaws or obstacles.

Negative change arcs depict characters who devolve, becoming worse versions of themselves.

Flat arcs feature characters who remain true to their core values and beliefs throughout the story but influence the world around them.

Character Development

Begin with a well-developed character with strengths, weaknesses, motivations, and flaws. Understand their starting point in terms of their personality, beliefs, and values.

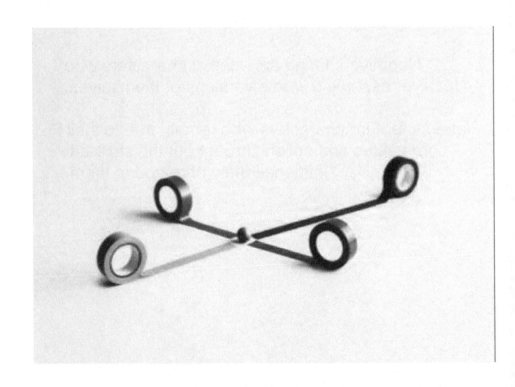

Identify the Character's Goal or Need

Determine what the character wants or needs to achieve by the end of the story. This goal or need will be the driving force behind their arc.

The character's goal should be specific, tangible, and related to their personal growth or the story's central conflict.

Create Obstacles and Conflict

Introduce obstacles and conflicts that challenge the character's beliefs, values, or flaws. These challenges should make it difficult for the character to achieve their goal.

The character's journey should involve both internal conflicts (emotional and psychological) and external conflicts (physical and situational).

Show Progression and Change

Throughout the story, depict the character's progression, setbacks, and changes in behaviour, beliefs, or attitudes.
Highlight key moments where the character learns, adapts, or makes pivotal decisions that contribute to their arc.

Use Inner Monologue and Dialogue

Utilize inner monologue to reveal the character's evolving thoughts, doubts, and self-reflection. Show how their internal struggles impact their decisions.

Engage in meaningful dialogue that reflects the character's growth or resistance to change. Dialogues with other characters can expose their evolving perspectives.

Show Consequences

Illustrate the consequences of the character's choices and actions, both positive and negative. Consequences can drive the character's growth or intensify their internal conflicts.

Foreshadow and Symbolism

Use foreshadowing and symbolism to hint at the character's potential arc. These literary devices can create anticipation and deeper meaning in the story.

Resolution and Transformation

In the story's resolution, demonstrate how the character has changed, evolved, or resolved their internal conflicts in response to the obstacles and challenges they've faced.

Ensure that the character's transformation aligns with the story's themes and messages.

Consistency and Authenticity

Maintain consistency in the character's development. Their arc should be organic and believable based on their established traits and experiences.

Ensure that the character's transformation is authentic and not forced for the sake of the plot.

Reader Empathy and Connection

Craft the character arc in a way that allows readers to empathize with the character's struggles and growth. A well-executed character arc can make the reader emotionally invested in the story.

Beta Readers and Feedback

Share your work with beta readers or writing groups to gather feedback on the effectiveness of the character arc and its impact on the story.

By following these steps and considering the unique needs of your characters and story, you can create compelling character arcs that enhance the depth and emotional resonance of your narrative. Character arcs provide a powerful tool for exploring themes, conveying messages, and engaging readers on a profound level.

How characters change and evolve throughout the narrative.
Characters change and evolve throughout a narrative as a result of their experiences, challenges, and the choices they make. This transformation is a fundamental element of storytelling, adding depth and complexity to characters. Here's an explanation of how characters change and evolve over the course of a narrative:

Initial State and Traits

Characters are introduced to readers or viewers with certain personality traits, beliefs, values, strengths, and weaknesses. This initial state serves as a baseline for their development.

Motivation or Goal

Characters often have a motivation, goal, or need they wish to fulfil. This goal could be personal, relational, professional, or related to the central conflict of the story.

Conflict and Challenges

As the story unfolds, characters encounter obstacles, conflicts, and challenges that prevent them from easily achieving their goals. These hurdles can be external (e.g., a villain, a physical obstacle) or internal (e.g., self-doubt, inner conflicts).

Choices and Decisions

Characters' choices and decisions in response to these challenges drive their development. These choices can be motivated by a desire to overcome obstacles, fulfil their goals, or adapt to changing circumstances.

Congratulations on completing this course! You now have the skills and knowledge to create compelling characters that resonate with your readers and elevate your storytelling to new heights. Get ready to embark on a journey of character exploration and development!

Printed in Great Britain
by Amazon

28232189R00046